Where is Simon, Sandy? is dedicated to
the children of
The Turks and Caicos Islands.

All proceeds will be donated to
The Children's Programme
of The Turks and Caicos National Museum.

Turks and Caicos
National Museum

WHERE IS SIMON, SANDY?

The story of a little donkey that wouldn't quit
(Based on a true story)

Donna Marie Seim
Illustrated by Susan Spellman

PublishingWorks, Inc.
Exeter, NH

Turks and Caicos National Museum
Turks and Caicos Islands, BWI
2008

On an island called Grand Turk, surrounded by a turquoise sea, lived an old man named Simon, and his little donkey, Sandy.

Simon lived in a small stone cottage with a red tin roof. Sandy slept in a cozy shed that Simon had built especially for her. Simon shared his cottage with Blackie the cat, and his yard with Bupper the rooster, and some very chatty hens.

The gate from Simon's yard led the way down the winding path to Cockburn Town.

Every morning when the sun peaked above the sea, Simon hitched Sandy up to a cart full of empty pails, and led her to the well. Simon then dipped each pail into the fresh, cold water, as Sandy stood, waiting, until all the pails were brimming full. Sandy knew exactly how long it took Simon to fill the pails. At just the right time, she began to walk the winding road to Cockburn Town.

The little donkey loved her job. At the red gate Sandy waited for Simon to deliver the water and return the empty pail. Simon didn't have to tell Sandy when to move on to the blue gate or the yellow gate. Sandy knew the way.

At the end of each day when Simon and Sandy returned home, Blackie would purr, Bupper would crow and flap his wings, and the chatty hens would run around in circles. Simon would reward Sandy with a pail of her own fresh water, some tasty hay, and a crunchy carrot. Sandy loved her crunchy carrots!

One morning, as the sun rose hot above the sea, Simon did not come out of his cottage to hook Sandy to her cart. Sandy left her shed and paced back and forth in front of the cottage, braying for Simon to come out.

Bupper crowed, and the chatty hens clucked, but neither Simon nor Blackie came out of the cottage.

Where was Simon? It was time to go to work! Sandy walked to the well without Simon and without her cart. She waited the exact amount of time that Simon would have needed to fill all the pails with water. Then she nudged the gate open and walked the winding path to town, alone. Sandy arrived at the red gate and stopped. She waited the exact amount of time that Simon would need to deliver the water. She walked to the blue gate and waited, then she walked on to the yellow gate.

Children were playing in the front of their house when they saw Sandy come up to the yellow gate. "Where is Simon, Sandy?" the children called to the little donkey. Sandy shook her head and walked on.

The children followed Sandy. They stopped at each gate when Sandy stopped, and called to the other children to come out and follow Sandy, too.

When they reached the center of town the baker saw Sandy and the parade of children. "Where is Simon, Sandy?" he called to the little donkey.

Sandy shook her head and walked on.

When they passed the clothing store, the storekeeper saw Sandy and the parade of children. "Where is Simon, Sandy?" she called to the little donkey.

Sandy shook her head and walked on.

When Sandy came to the very last gate she stopped and the children stopped, too. This was the village doctor's house. The doctor looked out of his window and saw all the children. He saw Sandy waiting at his gate. He grabbed his doctor's bag and ran outside.

"Where is Simon, Sandy?" he asked the little donkey.

Sandy shook her head and walked the winding road up to Simon's stone cottage.

The doctor and the parade of children followed close behind her.

Sandy brayed for Simon to come out. The doctor knocked on the door.

A weak voice said, "Come in." When the doctor opened the door he saw Simon sitting on the floor with his foot raised up on a stack of pillows.

"Simon, what happened?" the doctor asked.

"I got up in the middle of the night to get a glass of water and tripped over Blackie and hurt my foot," Simon said. "Blackie is hurt, too."

The doctor opened his black bag and pulled out a long bandage and a small one.

The doctor rolled the long bandage round and round Simon's foot. He wrapped the small one around Blackie's paw.

"Now, you must stay off of your foot until it mends!" warned the doctor.

"But who will deliver the water to all the people in Cockburn Town?" Simon asked.

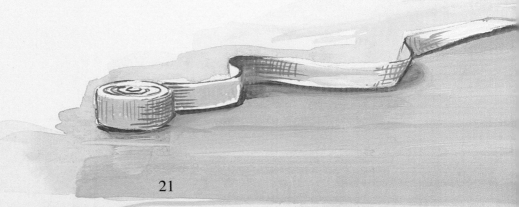

"Sandy will deliver the water to all the people in Cockburn Town," the children sang through the window.

"But who will hitch Sandy to her cart and pour the water from the well into the pails?" Simon asked.

"We will hitch Sandy to her cart and we will pour the water from the well into the pails," the children sang through the window.

"But who will feed Sandy her fresh water, her tasty hay, and crunchy carrot?" Simon asked.

"We will feed Sandy her fresh water, her tasty hay, and crunchy carrot," the children sang through the window.

"Sandy can deliver the water," the good doctor said.

"She knows the way!" the children sang through the window.

For the next week the children came
every morning when the sun peaked above
the sea. They hitched Sandy to her cart, and
walked her to the well. They filled all the pails
brimming with water. Then Sandy led the way
to town, stopping at the red gate, the blue
gate, and then the yellow gate. The people
in Cockburn Town waited by their gates for
Sandy and the children to come. The children
carried the pails of water to each house,
returning the empty pails to Sandy's cart. And
everyone waited for Simon's foot to mend.

Then one day Simon said to the children, "My foot is all mended." Simon was eager to get back to his work. He did not need the help of the children any longer. The children were glad that Simon's foot was better. But they all had sad faces. Even Sandy hung her head.

Simon smiled and said, "All right, you may come along with Sandy and me today!"

The children cheered, but the next day, they looked sad again, so Simon said the children could come along once more. And then again the next day, and the next, and every day after that!

And so, if you come to this special island in the Caribbean, look for an old man, his little donkey, and a cart full of pails brimming with water.

And following behind them, a parade of children singing and dancing!

29

Author's Note

Where is Simon, Sandy? is based on a true story about a little donkey that wouldn't quit. The donkey and her master delivered the water everyday to the people of Cockburn Town, on the island of Grand Turk. She knew the way by heart. When her master was no longer able to deliver the water, she walked the route, without her cart, alone. She went to each and every gate and waited just the right amount of time it would take to deliver a pail of water. The little donkey did this everyday for the rest of her life!

To understand the story it helps to know that the island of Grand Turk is a desert-like island with very little rainfall. The people did not have running water or plumbing as they do today. Instead they had to catch the rainwater with large basins or tubs as it ran off of their roofs. Water was more precious than gold. The people on Grand Turk were lucky to have two natural fresh water wells but they were located quite a distance from town. There were no trucks or cars back then, so it was a long hot walk to the well and back. The pails filled with water were very heavy to carry. Have you ever tried carrying a pail of water on your head? Donkeys pulling carts were able to transport many pails of the much-needed water from the well into town.

How did donkeys come to live on this island in the Caribbean? They were brought by boat with the people who came to harvest the salt from the sea. The people who came to the salt islands of Grand Turk, South Caicos and Salt Cay were from the island of Bermuda. These early settlers channeled the water from the sea through canals into natural depressions in the middle of the island called salinas. Once in the salina, the water would begin to evaporate in the hot Caribbean sun leaving the sea salt to dry, forming beautiful white crystals. After the salt was completely dried it would be shoveled onto donkey carts and the donkeys would pull the carts to large barrels near the dock. Here the salt would be stored until it was loaded onto big ships to be sent to the United States and Europe. After 300 years the salt business on the salt islands began to decline. Modern technology of mining the salt took the place of the old way of harvesting salt from the sea.

If you would like to learn more about the Turks and Caicos Islands and its history you can visit the Turks and Caicos National Museum, located on Front Street in Grand Turk. Or visit the museum online at www.tcmuseum.org.

Turks and Caicos
National Museum

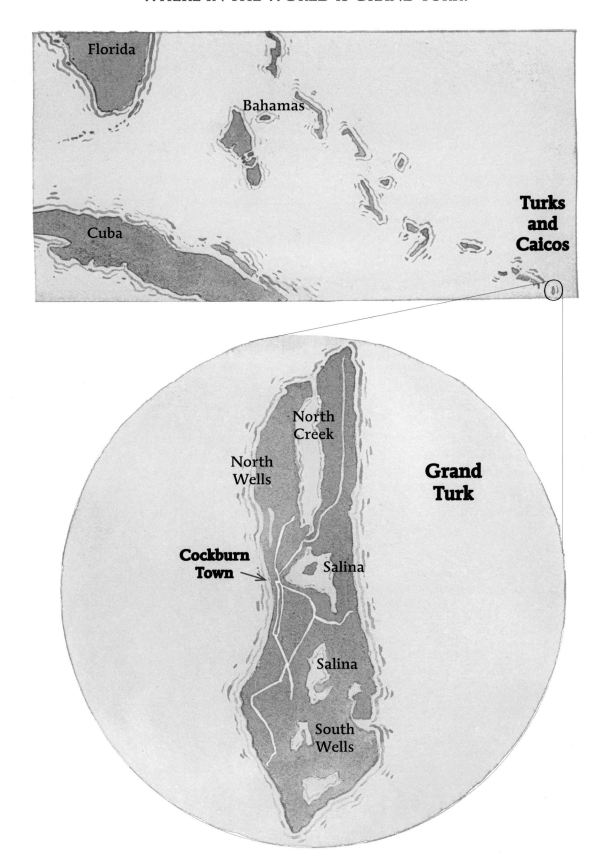

SOME FUN FACTS ABOUT DONKEYS

The earliest donkeys lived in Africa.
They looked like a zebra without stripes.
Sometimes today you can find a donkey with just one stripe.
Donkeys have long ears so they can hear faraway.
They have small but sturdy feet that are good for climbing.
The donkey cart was one of the very first ways to carry things and people.

Donkeys like people.
They make very good pets and will be loyal and true to their owners.
Donkeys are very smart.
They are easy to train if you are patient and kind to them.
Donkeys aren't always stubborn!
But they do like to do the same thing over and over again.

Donkeys eat grass and leafy green plants.
They like to eat flowers too, so keep your gates closed!
The mother donkey shows the young ones what is good for them to eat.
A baby donkey is called a foal.
A boy donkey is called a jack and a girl donkey is called a jenny or mare.
Donkeys have a very loud bray, or hee-haw, that can be heard from far away.

About the Author

Donna is a graduate of Ohio State University and holds a master's degree in Special Education from Lesley University. Donna's love of children and children's literature has played an integral role in her life. Her years working as a childcare worker and a special needs teacher were richly rewarding ones. In 1982, Donna and her husband Martin opened a specialty toy store, The Dragon's Nest. The store is now owned and operated by their daughter Kristin, allowing Donna the time to travel and to write. In her first book, *Fifty Cents an Hour,* she tells her childhood stories. She has just completed her first novel for children, *Hurricane Mia,* and is working on her second, *Charley!*

In, *Where is Simon, Sandy?* Donna brings to print a folktale that has been passed down by word of mouth for generations. The story brings to life the charm of The Turks and Caicos Islands and its people. Donna fell in love with these beautiful islands on her first visit over thirty-three years ago. She and her husband reside, with their dog Rags, in their country home in Newbury, Massachusetts. They travel often to Grand Turk having lovingly restored an island house, with a tin roof to catch the rain!

You can visit Donna at www.donnaseim.com.

About the Illustrator

Susan has a studio workshop in Newburyport, MA, where she pursues a dual career as a fine artist and as an illustrator with extensive experience in painting, portraiture, and children's book illustration.

Susan has illustrated stories for children's magazines, such as Highlights for Children and Cricket and for anthologies such as A Treasury of Christmas Tales and A Treasury of Bedtime Stories.

Her previous book for children was *How Timbo and Trevor Got Together* written by Barbara Towle. She also illustrated *Pinky and Bubs Stinky Night Out*, a story about two baby skunks and all the trouble they get into one summer night.

In addition to commercial art, Susan continues to pursue her interest in fine art. She paints regularly in oil with the "Newburyport Ten" Plein Air Painters and is a member of the Bridge Gallery, the Women in the Wild painters, and the Newburyport Art Association.

Her work can be viewed at www.suespellmanstudio.com.

First Edition 2008

Published in cooperation with the
Turks and Caicos National Museum
Guinep House, Front Street
Grand Turk
Turks and Caicos Islands
British West Indies
Tel & Fax +1 649-946-2160
Website: www.tcmuseum.org

PublishingWorks, Inc.,
60 Winter Street
Exeter, NH 03833
603-778-9883
www.publishingworks.com

PublishingWorks, Inc.

For Sales and Orders:

1-800-738-6603 or 603-772-7200

Designed by: Kat Mack and Susan Spellman

LCCN: 2008922363

ISBN: 1-933002-73-5

ISBN-13: 978-1-933002-73-6

I would like to thank Bryan Naqqi Manco, Conservation Officer from The Turks and Caicos National Trust, who told me the original folklore story. My sincere thanks to Deborah Annema, Programme Director of The Turks and Caicos National Museum, whose undying enthusiasm and support helped to get this book published. And to Patricia Saxton, who donated all her time and energy to solicit the funding to make, *Where is Simon, Sandy?* a reality.

I would also like to thank Susan Spellman for capturing the charm of the people and the islands in her exquisite colorful illustrations. And all the folks at PublishingWorks who have been a joy to work with through all the stages of making a folktale into a timeless book that can be passed on for generations.

— Donna

I would like to thank Donna Seim for giving me the opportunity to illustrate this wonderful story. I also thank PublishingWorks for being so great to work with. I would like to dedicate the book to my husband Jay, and my daughters Tina, Carey and Emily.

— Susan